A TRUMPET CLUB SPECIAL EDITION

To Barbara

Published by The Trumpet Club
666 Fifth Avenue, New York, New York 10103

Copyright © 1985 by Jack Kent

ISBN 0-440-84523-8

This edition published by arrangement with Simon and Schuster
Books for Young Readers, a division of Simon & Schuster, Inc.
Printed in the United States of America
November 1991

10 9 8 7 6 5 4 3 2 1
UPC

"Joey, come clean up your room!" mother kangaroo
said. "I've told you a hundred times!"
"Eight times," Joey mumbled. He had kept count.

Like all kangaroo children, Joey lived in his mother's pocket. At the moment, though, everything was in a jumble. There was hardly room for Joey to turn around.

Joey sighed and went to clean up his room.

But he took one look at the mess and decided
it would be easier to run away from home.

So he did.

"You're being awfully quiet, Joey," mother
said after a while. "Have you finished
cleaning your room?"
There wasn't any answer.

"Joey?" mother called. She looked
in her pocket to see what he was up to.
But he was nowhere in sight.

"He's hiding! The rascal! I'll find him!" said mother.

But Joey wasn't
under the bed.

And he wasn't
behind the dresser.

He wasn't ANYWHERE!

Mother saw a small piece of paper.
It was a note written in crayon. The note
said, "I hav runned away. Goodby. Joey."

"Joey's gone!" said mother,
and she started to cry.
Then she set out
to look for Joey.

Word soon got around that Joey's mother
had an empty room.

Several folks came to ask about the room.
"It's not for rent!" said mother.

But they looked it over.

And they tried it out.

And they decided it wasn't quite right
for any of them anyway.
"It's JOEY'S room!" said mother.

Meanwhile, Joey was trying to find a new place to live.

Every kangaroo mother's pocket was already filled.

But Joey found a pelican
whose pouch was empty.

And he moved in.

It was very comfortable.
But sometimes...

it was rather scary.

Joey decided to look some more.

When the postman started his rounds the next day,
he noticed that his mail pouch seemed heavier
than usual.

As he bounced along, Joey thought that
it wasn't like mother's pocket at all.
He was homesick.

It was late in the afternoon when the postman
delivered the mail to Joey's mother.
"A few bills," said the postman as he handed them
to her. "A letter. A magazine. Some junk mail.

"And, oh, yes! I think THIS is yours,"
he said, lifting Joey out of the pouch.

"Where have you been?" mother asked between
hugs and kisses.
"I was looking for a place to live," said Joey.

"Well, it just so happens that I have an empty
room," said mother. "See what you think of it."

Joey hopped right in. He was very happy
to be home again.
"It's just right!" he said.

"It only needs to be cleaned up a little,"
Joey said.
And he got right to work.